BIONICLE ®

The Final Battle

by Greg Farshtey

SCHOLASTIC INC.
New York Toronto London Auckland Sydney
Mexico City New Delhi Hong Kong Buenos Aires

For Peggy, who wins every battle with kindness

No part of this publication may be reproduced, stored in a retrieval system, or transmitted in any form or by any means, electronic, mechanical, photocopying, recording, or otherwise, without written permission of the publisher. For information regarding permission, write to Scholastic Inc., Attention: Permissions Department, 557 Broadway, New York, NY 10012.

ISBN-13: 978-0-545-08079-8
ISBN-10: 0-545-08079-7
LEGO, the LEGO logo, and BIONICLE
are trademarks of The LEGO Group. © 2008 The LEGO Group.
All rights reserved. Published by Scholastic Inc.
SCHOLASTIC and associated logos are trademarks and/or registered trademarks of Scholastic Inc.

12 11 10 9 8 7 6 5 4 3 2 1   8 9 10 11 12 13/0

Printed in the U.S.A.
First printing, November 2008

PROLOGUE

What Has Gone Before . . .

Long ago, when the universe was still being born, the Great Beings realized that it required a core from which all energies would flow. In their great wisdom, they created a massive chamber that would provide power eternal for the Great Spirit Mata Nui and the universe he would rule. They named this chamber "Karda Nui," the Matoran phrase meaning "Great Heart."

The place they created was more than just another cavern — it was so vast as to almost be a universe of its own. Barren desert stretched for hundreds of miles in every direction, and the roof of Karda Nui was so high above the ground it could barely be seen. But the universe core was incomplete, flawed, and much work had to be done before it would serve its purpose.

1

A tribe of Av-Matoran — villagers imbued with the power of Light — were sent to complete the last tasks required to prepare the core. Their labors were long and dangerous, as sentient energy beings called avohkah struck at random and killed or injured many Matoran. The crisis grew so great that a team of new heroes, the Toa Mata, were sent to Karda Nui to keep the villagers safe.

These Toa — Tahu, Gali, Pohatu, Onua, Lewa, and Kopaka — were raw and inexperienced. Still, they managed to use their wits and elemental powers to beat back the avohkah long enough for the Av-Matoran to finish their work. As the Matoran left Karda Nui, the Mata's true mission was revealed: They would spend thousands of years in the Codrex, a dome inside Karda Nui, waiting to be called should Mata Nui be struck down. Sleeping within Toa canisters, millennia would go by without their even knowing. The canisters would also serve to protect them from the awesome energy storm that would rage when Karda Nui first became active.

Time passed. Moisture caused great stalactites to form on the roof of the cave. Within that roof, Av-Matoran civilization flourished, protected from predators and anyone else who might wish them harm. And the Toa Mata slept on. . . .

Then, slightly over 1,000 years ago, disaster struck. The Brotherhood of Makuta attacked the Great Spirit Mata Nui, sending him into an unending slumber. The Toa Mata's canisters were launched in an effort to save him, but a malfunction would keep the Toa asleep for another millennium. A massive quake rocked the universe, causing the stalactites — and the Matoran who lived above — to fall. Worse still, a hole opened in the roof of Karda Nui and water from outside began to pour in. The sands below were turned into a swamp.

The surviving Av-Matoran built new villages on the tops of the stalactites, which were now impaled in the ground. They lived in peace and harmony in their new home. A thousand years passed this way until the Matoran had almost forgotten how to fear anything.

All that changed mere days ago. Dark, bat-winged shapes appeared in the skies over Karda Nui. They were powerful members of the Brotherhood of Makuta, and they used creatures called shadow leeches to corrupt many Matoran of Light. Soon, only one village survived, and it was only a matter of time before it too fell.

Salvation arrived in the form of Tahu and his team — transformed into more powerful Toa Nuva — who fought the Makuta in the sky and in the swamp. Now, with time running out for the universe, both sides are preparing for what will be the final battle.

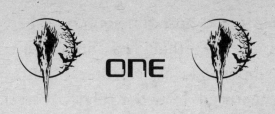

ONE

Tahu Nuva skimmed just above the swamp waters of Karda Nui, every sense on alert. He had been locked in aerial combat with Makuta Vamprah, until that bat-winged hunter vanished into the mists. Now it was a lethal game of hide-and-seek as he waited for the inevitable attack.

He found himself almost envying Pohatu, Kopaka, and Lewa, who had appeared from above with Matoran riding on their backs. A second set of eyes would have been welcome right about now.

There was a quick flash of shadow on the muddy water. Tahu rolled in midair and unleashed a stream of fireballs above and behind him. But there was no sign of an enemy, just empty sky.

Take it easy, Tahu told himself. *This is no worse than walking blindfolded through a Bohrok nest.*

He could hear the sounds of battle from far ahead. The other Toa Nuva were fighting with Vamprah's fellow Makuta, with most of the action centered around a spherical structure in the swamp called the Codrex. The Toa had been told that they had to get in there, for it held their "beginning and probable ending." The heroes possessed all six pieces of the keystone that would allow them access, but so far, had not been able to fight their way past the Makuta and get inside.

Tahu heard a soft whistle, as if something was falling nearby, followed by a harsh *click*. He had come to hate that noise. It was the sound of a Tridax pod opening up to unleash its cargo of shadow leeches. One leech could drain the light out of a Toa, Matoran, or any other being, leaving them a dark and corrupted pawn of the Makuta.

He glanced up. The four creatures were falling fast and right at him. It was too late to dodge, but not too late to trigger the power of his Hau Nuva mask. The Mask of Shielding threw a field of energy around him that kept the leeches from striking him. Amazingly, they attached themselves to the shield itself! Tahu shuddered at the sight of the disgusting beasts trying in vain to feed off the mask's energies.

Diving as close to the swamp water as he dared, he abruptly shut the shield off. The leeches tumbled into the water, which began to froth. Toa Onua had been the first to discover that the water was mutagenic, able to transform anything exposed to it. That was why the Toa avoided it at all costs. Now the shadow leeches were being changed ... probably something worse than what they were before. Tahu had no wish to hang around and see what that would be.

He caught a glimpse of Lewa, Onua, and Kopaka on a patch of ground up ahead, pinned down by shadow bolts fired by the Makuta Gali and Pohatu were caught up in their own battles, so any help was going to have to come from him.

So it's time to take care of my Makuta

problem, he decided. *Good thing I love the smell of burnt bat in the morning. . . .*

"You know," said Lewa Nuva, Toa of Air, "this reminds me of a story."

He, Kopaka Nuva, and Onua Nuva had their backs to a stand of trees in the swamp of Karda Nui. They were alternating firing their weapons and hurling elemental power at the attacking Makuta.

"Dare I hope it's one that doesn't end with six dead Toa Nuva?" joked Onua.

"Please tell me it's not the one about the three Matoran, the Manas crab, and the bucket," said Kopaka. "Last time you told me that, it took me a week to get the picture out of my head."

"No, no," Lewa replied, using a mini-cyclone to send four shadow leeches flying in opposite directions. "It's the one about the three Matoran, the Nui-Rama swarm, and the carry-basket of bula berries."

Onua glanced at Kopaka, even as a shadow

bolt splintered the tree behind him. "I don't think I know that one."

Kopaka shook his head. "I am sure I am going to regret this, but neither do I."

"Once, there were three Matoran," Lewa began.

Kopaka cut him off. "Is this really the time?"

"Once, there were three Matoran," Lewa repeated, more firmly. "They had gone out for a quick-walk to gather bula berries for dinner. Suddenly, they were attacked by a swarm of Nui-Rama. They were outnumbered and certain-doomed!"

"I don't need to hear this story," grumbled Kopaka. "I'm living it."

"But notice the Makuta are keeping their distance," chuckled Onua. "They must have heard Lewa tell a story before."

"As I was speak-saying," continued Lewa. "The Matoran were trapped, with no way out. Finally one of them said, 'I think they want the bula berries. Let's just give the berries to them.'

Well, everyone thought this was an ever-fine idea — better to be hungry than dead."

"I am still waiting for the part where heroic Toa Lewa saves the day," said Kopaka, battering a flight of shadow Matoran with an ice storm.

"So they left the basket of bula berries and backed away," Lewa continued, ignoring Kopaka. "And the Nui-Rama quick-flew down to it. But the next second, they started fighting among themselves over who would get the juicy berries. Before too long, there were no Nui-Rama left! So the three Matoran came out of hiding, took their berries, and went home."

"And the moral of the story is . . . ?" asked Onua.

"Travel with berries," said Kopaka.

Lewa sighed. "No, no . . . the key to beating the Nui-Rama was figuring out what they wanted. What do the Makuta want here?"

"I've been asking myself the same question," admitted Onua.

"It's obvious," said Kopaka. "They want

the six keystones that can be used to open the Codrex."

The Toa of Ice pointed to the large structure a few hundred yards away. It was protected by a field of energy so strong that even touching it sent one flying halfway across the swamp.

"Doesn't make sense," said Onua, summoning a wall of earth to block a Makuta lightning bolt. "The Brotherhood was here for days before we were, and they knew about the keystones. If they wanted in, they could have gotten in before we arrived. No, they have something else in mind, and I can prove it."

"How?" asked Lewa.

Onua pointed to the six Makuta in the air, each possessed with incredible power far outclassing any Toa. "Simple — we're not dead yet."

High above, Makuta Krika surveyed the battle raging all around him. It was a seesaw contest, with the Makuta driving the Toa back, and then the Toa mounting a spirited counterattack. An outsider viewing the conflict might think it could go on forever, but Krika knew it would not.

And that is what worries me, he thought. *Not whether we will win or lose here in this pesthole, but what happens when the battle is over. What kind of universe will remain? Would we be doing the Toa a favor by sparing their lives here, or committing the worst possible crime against them?*

A powerful jet of water passed through Krika's intangible form, doing him no harm. He turned to see Toa Gali flying toward him, her ghost blaster ready to fire. If the Toa expected cries of rage or shouts of defiance from Krika, though, she was disappointed.

"Must we dance this dance, Toa?" asked the Makuta. "You may not know how it must end, but I do."

"Then let me in on the secret," Gali said, firing her blaster. Bars of energy appeared from thin air around the Makuta.

"There is an old saying on the island of Zakaz," Krika replied. "Only a fool fights in a burning forest. While you waste your time battling us, your universe is burning to the ground, little Toa."

Krika suddenly passed through the bars and shot forward. Before Gali could react, he had turned solid and grabbed her, draining some of her energy in the process. "Come with me," said the Makuta, steering her flight away from the battle, "and I will tell a tale that will freeze your heart and turn your hopes to ashes."

Pohatu saw Gali being carried off, but was in no position to help. He had been slugging it out with Makuta Gorast for what seemed like an eternity. So far, she had plowed her way through a hail of light spheres, shrugged off boulders, and survived direct hits by uprooted trees. He had even flown around her at super-speed, delivering a thousand blows in a second, and done little more than shake her up.

"Fall down already," the Toa of Stone grumbled. "You're making me all frustrated."

Gorast's response was an amused hiss, followed by a crushing blow that sent Pohatu and his Matoran companion, Photok, flying toward the Codrex. When they struck the energy field, they were hurled in the opposite direction, right toward Gorast. She met them with another blow. They crashed down into the mud and lay there, barely moving.

"Toa of Stone," Gorast laughed. "Toa of Clay would seem more accurate. Did you truly think you could stand against a warrior who has ground armies beneath her heel?"

Pohatu painfully raised his head out of the mire and wiped mud from his mask. "Well, it seemed like — *ow!* — a good idea at the time."

"You Toa Nuva will die here," Gorast continued, floating closer to the fallen pair. "And the Matoran will join with us in darkness. The Plan will go forward. You cannot stop it."

Pohatu made it to his hands and knees. Beside him, Photok was stirring. "Wouldn't dream of it. But maybe you should tell me what this big Plan is, so I can make sure I don't get in its way."

Gorast smiled. "I have a better idea," she said, reaching out to touch Pohatu's armor and triggering her Mask of Disruption at the same time.

Instantly, the Toa felt his elemental power building up inside of him. Then it was being released against his will, flowing out of him and creating stone all around. Within moments, he and Photok were buried by a ton of rock, then two tons, then three, with no end in sight. The sheer weight carried them down into the swamp inside a shell of stone, the product of a Toa's power gone wild.

"You Toa truly are remarkable," Gorast said, watching as the rock vanished from view beneath the mud. "It is not every being who can create their own tomb."

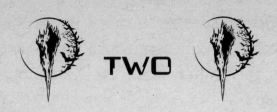

TWO

"We were not always like this, you know," Krika said, with something in his voice that Gali never thought she would hear from a Makuta: regret.

The Toa of Water was still feeling weak and dizzy from Krika's attack. She did her best to ignore it. One of her strengths had always been the ability to listen and to try to understand both her friends and her enemies. She had a chance to do that now with this Makuta, and she wasn't going to blow it.

"I know," she replied. "The swamp water must have mutated —"

Krika shook his head, sadly. "I'm not talking about how we look. I'm talking about what we are. A piece of advice, Toa — if you keep focusing only on the now, there isn't going to be any later."

The Final Battle

The Makuta turned ghostly and floated up off the ground. "There was a time, back when Makuta Miserix led us, that the Brotherhood stood for something. Oh, you would not remember him — you were asleep at the time — but he embraced our true mission. Under his guidance, we created Rahi beasts that are still of use to the Matoran today. When the Matoran civil war happened on Metru Nui, it was Miserix who decreed we Makuta must get more involved in the world outside our laboratories." He paused for a moment, then added, "That was the beginning of the end."

Gali knew the rest of the story all too well. The Brotherhood rebelled against the Great Spirit Mata Nui, casting him into an unending sleep and plunging the universe into a time of darkness. The mission of the Toa Nuva was to undo that criminal act and awaken Mata Nui once more.

"When we saw the universe beyond our towers, we discovered how Mata Nui was honored, respected, and loved by the Matoran," said

Krika. "That was love and devotion we felt we deserved for the thousands of things we had done to better their lives. Jealousy turned to resentment, and resentment to hate. And when Makuta Teridax proposed we strike at Mata Nui and seize power, we turned away from Miserix and followed his lead."

"And what happened to Miserix?" asked Gali. She could feel her strength returning. If she could keep Krika talking, she would soon be able to make a break for freedom.

"Teridax wanted to kill him," Krika replied. "Makuta Spiriah and I were given the job, but Spiriah didn't have the stomach for killing mask to mask. I told him I would handle it . . . but instead, I brought Miserix to a volcanic island in the south and imprisoned him there."

"So you disobeyed," said Gali. "I didn't think Makuta had the spines to do that."

Krika shrugged, sending a strange ripple of motion through his intangible form. "Perhaps we do not," he said quietly. "Should the volcanoes erupt with enough force and for enough time,

Miserix will have no hope of survival. I gave him a chance, that's all."

Gali said nothing. She was remembering how Tahu and Kopaka had been dispatched by the Order of Mata Nui to stop a series of volcanic eruptions on a southern island, shortly before the team came to Karda Nui. Could it have been the same place that Miserix was imprisoned? Was that why the Order wanted the eruptions blocked?

"As I now give you one," said Krika. He pushed something toward her through the mud. Gali picked it up and used the slightest bit of her elemental power to wash the soil away. She saw it was a piece of stone, about the size of her hand, with the symbol of the Brotherhood of Makuta engraved on it.

"With that, anyone — even you — can pass unharmed through the forces of the Brotherhood," Krika continued. "Take it. I will lead you to an exit from this place. Return to Metru Nui, Xia, anywhere that is not here. Just go, Gali, if you value your universe."

Gali was surprised at the urgency in his voice, but unconvinced by his plea. "If you want me gone, why not just kill me? You have the power."

Krika smiled. The expression gave Gali chills. "The Makuta have a legend. It says that when one of us dies, all that we have put out into the universe comes back to us. For tens of thousands of years, I have put fear, pain, and death out into the universe, Toa. Perhaps I want to add a strain of mercy to that mix."

Gali studied the Makuta. Was this a trick? Some attempt to weaken the Toa's ranks? None of it made sense.

"Why?" she said finally. "Why do you want me gone? Or is it that you simply want one less Toa Nuva in Karda Nui?"

Krika laughed softly. It was a hollow and horrible sound, somehow worse to Gali's ears than a scream of rage would have been. "You should have been a Makuta, Gali, you are far too clever to be a mere Toa. You Nuva are here to awaken Mata Nui, a mission that requires all six of you. I tell you that if you do this, you and everything you know, everything you love, will be doomed to a future more horrible than you can imagine. Leave here now, and that future cannot come to pass."

Tahu racked his brain. Vamprah had proven impossible to shake and far more skilled at aerial combat than the Toa. Mere fire bolts weren't going to stop a Makuta who had a natural resistance to fire. Something much bigger was going to be needed.

Nova blast? No, that might harm my friends as well, thought Tahu. *I need something sudden, unexpected. . . .*

He glanced around, looking for something that would inspire an idea. He found it in a pile of rotting vegetation atop an islet of mud off to the east. They reminded him of something he had seen once in the swamps of Le-Wahi on the island of Mata Nui. Turaga Matau had said something about some of the plants on the island not being like those in Metru Nui. They didn't seem to be made of protodermis and didn't break down the same way when they died. Tahu realized that in the end they resembled these dead plants in Karda Nui.

It makes sense, thought the Toa of Fire. *Matau said some of the plants might have come from other islands. The plants here might have come in with the waters that flooded Karda Nui from outside. And he warned me not to use my powers around them when they started to rot, because . . .*

Tahu smiled. *Oh no. Wouldn't dream of it.*

He turned then and remained hovering in the air, not far from the decaying plant matter. Vamprah never hesitated, flying straight toward him, hungry for a fight. Tahu waited until Vamprah was just over the islet before tossing a fireball. But he didn't aim it at the Makuta — he aimed it at the plants.

As soon as the fire came near its target, there was a huge explosion of flame. The shock sent Vamprah reeling and even Tahu rolled through the air before finally regaining control. When he looked back, a shaken Vamprah was clinging to a tree, the only thing keeping him from plunging into the swamp.

Score one for swamp gas, Tahu said to himself. *One spark, and boom! I guess Matau was right after all.*

"Pohatu! Wake up!" Photok said frantically. He and the unconscious Toa were inside a tiny air pocket beneath tons of rocks. Already, the atmosphere was getting thin.

At first, the Av-Matoran thought he could use his light powers to blast their way free. But his first shot produced nothing but a rain of rubble. It was obvious they would be crushed to death long before that method of escape would work.

The Matoran shook the fallen Toa, but it did no good. Then he hit him with a little light blast, followed by a bigger one. When neither did the trick, he upped the power one more time. This time it worked, with Pohatu awakening so abruptly he almost crushed Photok against the rocks above.

"What? Where?" shouted Pohatu.

"If you would — *ow* — not flatten me, maybe I could tell you," grumbled Photok. "We have a problem. But a little speed like we used before and I bet we can fly right out of here —"

"And into the swamp water," Pohatu cut him off. "Onua warned me about that stuff. Maybe we'd be fast enough that it wouldn't affect us, but why take the chance? I've got a better idea."

Pohatu closed his eyes and lay perfectly still. Photok was going to ask just what in Mata Nui's name he was doing, but thought better of it. Maybe the Toa of Stone was concentrating, and it just *looked* like he was taking a nap. He decided to give it a few more seconds and see if anything happened.

That was when something did. First, Photok saw the rocks above and below fuse together into a solid mass. There was a sensation of motion, and the Matoran felt a little dizzy for a moment. Then he realized what was happening: He, Pohatu, and all the rock that surrounded them were rising. The Toa was using his mastery of stone to levitate them from the swamp at an amazing rate of speed. .

"Wish I had a Mask of X-Ray Vision right about now," Pohatu muttered. "I'd drop us right on Gorast."

The Toa felt the slightest decrease in resistance to their movement, which told him they were out of the water and back in the air. Making sure Photok was securely on his back, he unleashed his power and split their rocky prison wide open. Before the two halves had even hit the swamp, Toa and Matoran were soaring back into the battle.

Halfway to the Codrex, they were joined in flight by Tahu. "Have you seen Gali?" the Toa of Stone asked.

"No," answered Tahu, instantly concerned by the tone of his comrade's voice. "What happened?"

Pohatu explained how he had seen Krika carrying off the Toa of Water. In the past, Tahu would have ordered Pohatu into the fight while he went and searched for Gali. But time and experience had made him less a warrior and more a leader of Toa.

"You're fastest," Tahu said. "Go find her and bring her to the Codrex. I'll help the others and we'll meet you there. And, Pohatu . . ."

"Don't worry," said the Toa of Stone. "She's my friend, too, remember?"

Nodding, Tahu jetted toward the Codrex. Pohatu and Photok turned and headed in the opposite direction, both hoping against hope they would find the Toa of Water still alive.

High above the swamp, Ignika, the Toa of Life, stood guard over the fallen Makuta Icarax. Not long ago, Ignika had simply been a Mask of Power. Using its control over all life, it had fashioned a body for itself from the molecules in the swamp in an attempt to be a hero like the Toa.

It had not been easy. Ignika's first battles were awkward, and at one point he even clashed with the Toa Nuva. But when Icarax challenged him, Ignika defeated the powerful Makuta decisively. Now, in pain and barely conscious, the

Makuta looked up at Ignika with hatred in his eyes.

Icarax was a warrior. He had fought and won a thousand battles. Victory meant the death of the opponent, so the fact that Ignika had not yet killed him was, to Icarax, a sign of weakness. "Why do you hesitate?" he sneered. "Does the 'Toa of Life' not have the stomach to bring death?"

Ignika, puzzled, did not respond. He was not aware of the Toa code that prohibited killing, nor had he kept Icarax alive out of any sense of mercy or forgiveness. He simply didn't see Icarax as a threat, so not worth the effort of eliminating.

"Go ahead," said Icarax. "I'll only be beating everyone else here to nonexistence by a few hours."

Again, Ignika didn't react. The Makuta sat up and stared at his foe. Then Icarax's eyes widened and he began to laugh. "You don't know! The great Mask of Life doesn't even know what it is here for! Oh, this is too fine a joke!"

Icarax rose painfully to his feet. Ignika braced for another attack, but one wasn't coming. Instead, the Makuta pointed at the Mask of Life. "Look at your mask, Toa. Everyone knows the legend of the golden Mask of Life, but your mask isn't gold — it's silver with shades of black. Don't you know what that means? It means the end of everything."

Icarax laughed again, a sound heavy with malice and madness. "Makuta Teridax told us all about you. The Great Beings created you not only as a cure for what might ail Mata Nui. You were their way to fix any mistakes they might have made in the creation of this universe. If the universe is too far out of balance, a countdown begins. Your mask turns to silver . . . and then to black . . . and when it is as black as a Makuta's spirit, all life in this universe will cease to exist. All 'mistakes' will be erased, and the Great Beings, wherever they are, can start again somewhere else."

Toa Ignika knew very little about how to look for lies and deception. But even if he had, he would not have found any in Icarax's words. The Makuta was telling the truth, and somehow Ignika knew that. And that meant the Toa Nuva were racing a doomsday clock and didn't even know it!

Icarax forgotten, Toa Ignika climbed aboard his skyboard and rocketed down toward the swamp. The Nuva had to be warned before it was too late.

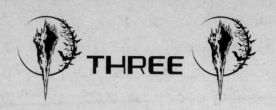

THREE

It had been two hours since Takanuva, Toa of Light, stumbled through a hole in space and fell face-first into the mud. After what he had just been through, even so messy and humiliating an arrival felt like a victory.

He had been traveling in between dimensions for what felt like an eternity. His journey had begun in the city of Metru Nui, courtesy of a damaged Great Mask worn by a being named Brutaka. His mission was to travel to Karda Nui and bring vital information to the Toa Nuva. But the ride had been a stormy one, and more than once he had wound up in strange, sometimes frightening alternate dimensions. Takanuva could only hope that this time he had finally reached his destination.

Since his arrival, he had been flying east, looking for some sign of the Toa Nuva. He had spotted figures flitting through the sky and what might have been battles, but he was too far away to make out clearly who they were or what was going on.

That was about to change. He spotted Gali Nuva on a spit of mud, being menaced by what looked like a giant insect with an attitude. Takanuva hesitated for just a moment — he had all too painfully learned the dangers of judging by appearance in recent adventures — but he couldn't escape the fact that Gali was lying on the ground and that thing was closing in on her.

Takanuva fired a warning blast of light in front of the insectoid's path. The being turned his head to look at the Toa, and Takanuva would forever remember the expression on his face. It wasn't fear or anger — more like sadness, as if the bone-white creature had finally accepted his fate.

The Toa of Light braced for an attack. Instead, the insectoid being turned ghostly and vanished into the ground. Gali got to her feet as

Takanuva joined her. The two spoke at the same time.

"How did you get here —?"

"Are you all right —?"

"It's a long story," said Takanuva. "Where are the others? I have news you need to hear."

Gali glanced down at the spot of ground into which Krika had disappeared. "They're back that way. Karda Nui is under attack by the Makuta, and —" She glanced up at Takanuva, eyes wide. "What happened to you? Your armor . . . your mask . . . and is it me, or are you bigger?"

"I don't know about the last," Takanuva said grimly. "But as for the rest — I'll tell you while we travel." He reached behind and took something off his back. Gali recognized it as a smaller version of the sundial Lewa had retrieved from the island of Mata Nui.

"What are you going to do with that?" she asked.

Takanuva put the sundial on the ground and then shot a beam of light at it from his left hand. The arrow on the sundial cast a shadow that pointed to the east. Takanuva had no way of knowing it, but it was pointing right toward the Codrex.

"Okay," he said softly. "So I still go that way."

Gali looked at him, thoroughly confused.

"I was told Lewa Nuva retrieved this from this island of Mata Nui not too long ago," the Toa of Light hurriedly explained. "It was shrunk down and given to me for my journey here. When I focus light upon it, the sundial points toward the spot from which the Great Spirit can be awakened."

Gali was going to ask more questions, but she was distracted by the arrival of Pohatu and Photok, who came to a landing in front of the two Toa. Pohatu looked Takanuva up and down for a few moments, finally saying, "Hmm. Can't say I think much of the color change."

"You should talk," Takanuva muttered. "You're orange!"

"Yeah," Pohatu smiled. "But I wear it well."

* * *

Makuta Mutran was extremely unhappy. The Toa Nuva had succeeded in destroying his original hive along with the vats he used to create shadow leeches. He had been forced to relocate his operations to an island in the swamp, using whatever extra equipment he'd had stored outside the hive. The situation was neither efficient nor ideal, especially to an "artist" like Mutran.

"Impossible," he growled. "I can't work in this mud pit! I can't create under these conditions!"

His Matoran assistant, Vican, stayed far away, knowing better than to even speak when Mutran was like this. Since the day he had been turned into a shadow Matoran and then mutated by his master, Vican had lived a life that could be compared to tiptoeing through a nest of sleeping doom vipers. He never knew what might inspire Mutran to toss him into a vat and see what new changes could be made.

Still, Vican couldn't help but be curious about today's project. Mutran was making some kind of winged, insectoid Rahi beast, but it wasn't at Antroz's request. And when Mutran did things on his own, the results were unpredictable.

Summoning his courage, Vican edged a little closer. "Um . . . great Mutran . . . what might that be?"

Mutran turned, surprised that Vican had dared to interrupt, but eager to show off his work. "That is a klakk. I made several very, very long ago — nasty little things, but excellent sentries. Since our new location is more exposed than the hive, I felt it might be of use. It should be ready to emerge from the vat soon."

Vican eyed the creature. It didn't look like it was going to follow Mutran's schedule. It was ramming against the side of the vat and cracks were starting to appear in the crystal. Mutran noticed and plunged his spear into the tank, trying to drive the Rahi back, but all that did was irritate the klakk. With a final thrust, it shattered the vat and burst free.

Mutran made a grab for it, but the klakk was too fast. It shot on a straight line for Vican, a horrible shriek coming from its mouth. The sound was so loud and sharp it felt like a physical blow. Vican was knocked off his feet and, for a few moments, the world went black.

The next thing he knew, Mutran was hauling him out of the mud. He felt strange and sick, but he wasn't going to show any sign of weakness to his master. His . . . master? Somehow, that didn't sound at all right.

"It flew off," snarled Mutran. "Go and bring it back!"

Vican could see the klakk, already well away from the island. He could see something else too. There were three Toa, one of whom he didn't recognize, flying in the same general direction. The sight made Vican hesitate.

There are a thousand other places these Toa could be right now, safe places, far away from this, he thought. *But they come here and risk their lives for Matoran they don't even know. And what have I done? Everything I could — no, everything I was told to do — to stop them.*

Vican took flight, moving more slowly than he normally would have. Something was happening inside him. He had never had any regrets about his actions, not since the day Mutran's shadow leech drained the light from him. Things like conscience and regret went with it, leaving just darkness behind. So why did he suddenly care about this place, these Toa and Matoran, now?

Troubled, he winged away, his mind full of questions.

The appearance of Takanuva was a surprise for both the other Toa Nuva and the Makuta. With his light power added to the battle, the Toa earned a victory, though at best a temporary one. The Makuta retreated toward the Codrex.

Tahu wasn't going to waste this time. He collected all six keystones that the Toa had collected and fitted them together. As the Matoran had told them, the inscriptions on the stone told how the Toa could awaken the Great Spirit Mata Nui.

Tahu read them over carefully, then had the others do the same. The process would be a long and complicated one, but not impossible. If they could hold the Makuta off long enough, they could awaken the Great Spirit and end the Brotherhood's dreams of conquest.

"We have to get into the Codrex," he said. "We have the keystone. Now we just have to get past the Makuta. Once we do that, we can start the awakening."

"Wait. You . . . must . . . wait."

The voice was harsh and raspy, as if the speaker had not used it in ages. The truth was Toa Ignika, who now hovered above the Toa, had never spoken aloud in all of his short existence in this form.

"What is it?" asked Onua. "What do you know?"

In halting, uncertain speech, Ignika told the Toa what Icarax had told him. "I hadn't realized before, but . . . it has changed color." Kopaka said. "Remember? When we talked with Axonn on the island of Voya Nui, he described it as a 'golden mask.'"

"Since when do Makuta tell the truth about anything?" asked Pohatu.

"Do you want to be the one who risks all on the notion they might be lying?" Kopaka replied.

"Then we move fast," said Tahu.

Gali read over the keystones again. "Tahu, we don't have any way of knowing how long we have before this . . . countdown . . . reaches its end. What if we can't complete this process in time?"

Now it was Takanuva's turn to speak up. "We have another problem. If we succeed in waking up the Great Spirit, all of this place is going to be hit with an energy storm so big it will kill everything in Karda Nui. If we don't get ourselves and the Matoran out of here in time . . ." There was no need to finish the statement.

"So if we fail, everyone quick-dies. And if we succeed, everyone quick-dies," said Lewa Nuva. "Oh, those Great Beings and their whacky sense of humor."

FOUR

"Eight of us, six of them," said Pohatu. "I like those odds."

The Toa, Takanuva, and Toa Ignika were assembled about half a mile from the Codrex. Of the Makuta guarding the structure, only Icarax and Mutran seemed to be missing. The rest were waiting impatiently for the Toa attack they knew would be coming.

"Surprise is out," said Tahu. "We hit them and hope some of us make it inside. Don't get tied down by individual fights. And if one of our own falls, keep moving. Don't stop. This may be our only shot at this."

"Hold on," said Kopaka. "They know we're coming, but not when, so maybe we should announce it. Consider this . . ."

When Kopaka was finished speaking, the Toa took their positions. Gali had to guide Ignika to his spot and remind him what it was he had to do and when. As the Mask of Life, Ignika had never had to worry about complicated battle plans in the past. That was left to the guardians the mask created for itself.

"All right," said Tahu. "Let's soften them up."

Lewa, Gali, and Takanuva struck first. Combining their powers, the Toa of Air and Water conjured a storm with deafening claps of thunder. At the same time, Takanuva used his light power to create a brilliant, blinding flash.

While the Makuta were still dealing with the assault of sound and light, Tahu used his power to turn one of the massive stalactites red hot. As soon as it glowed crimson, Pohatu brought it down in a rain of rubble on the assembled Makuta. Those who tried to fly out of the way were grabbed by hands of earth created by Onua and pulled down.

Now it was Kopaka's turn. He knew well the resistance to cold each Makuta had. But now he combined subzero chill with Toa Ignika's weakening of the Makuta's life force. The enemy was slowed, but not yet out.

"Go!" yelled Kopaka. All eight Toa shot forward, protected by Tahu's Mask of Shielding, elemental powers blasting in every direction. From the ground, Gorast fired a bolt of molecular disruption, shattering the Toa's shield.

"Separate!" ordered Tahu. The Toa immediately peeled off from their formation, each coming toward the Codrex from a different direction and peppering the Makuta with elemental energy. The Makuta fought back with chain lightning, heat vision, and sonic attack. Onua was the first to go down, hit by Bitil's power scream.

Seeing the Toa of Earth fall from the sky, Gali swerved toward him. She caught him just before he hit the swamp, then struggled to regain altitude while dodging cyclones created by Antroz. "Save yourself!" Onua shouted over the wind. "Those were Tahu's orders!"

"Sorry, brother," Gali said, smiling. "I can't hear you over this big breeze."

The Final Battle

The way ahead was littered with molten rock, tornadoes, lightning bolts, Matoran of Light locked in combat with Matoran of Shadow, and Makuta pursuing Toa. Gali dodged the cyclones much as she had once dodged waterspouts beneath the endless sea, her eyes locked on the Codrex.

Up ahead, Gorast had caught up to Toa Ignika and slashed deep into his armor. Ignika turned in midair and regarded her as if she were some interesting new form of creature he had found under a rock. Then he casually waved a hand in her direction. In response, the molten rock assembled itself into a giant, its flaming eyes fixed on Gorast. Even as the Makuta used her shattering power to reduce it to fragments, the giant caught her with a backhanded blow that sent the Makuta flying.

With the immediate threat dealt with, Ignika glanced down at his damaged armor. Employing only a minor surge of power, he repaired the armor. Then he glanced at the fallen Gorast, with an almost childlike rage. She had tried to harm him. If she so much as moved, he would do far worse to her.

"Toa-brother!" Lewa yelled, grabbing Ignika's arm.

Ignika turned to look at him. Was this another attack? No, this was the green one. Ignika liked green; it was the color of plant life. "What do you want?" he said, haltingly.

"We have to go!" Lewa replied, pulling Ignika along. "Now, while they're scattered!"

Tahu slammed the keystone into place, dropping the field around the Codrex. "Come on!" he yelled as loud as he could. The other Toa rocketed toward his voice. A door opened in the spherical structure, and the heroes stormed inside. When they were safely in, Tahu retrieved the keystone and darted in himself, even as the field re-established itself.

"Seal the door!" the Toa of Fire shouted. But the door had already sealed itself. Through a small window that formed in the door, they could see the Makuta circling the Codrex like hungry kavinika after a kill.

"What now?" asked Takanuva.

"Well, first we —" began Pohatu. He stopped when he realized he had to look up to see the Toa of Light. "Hey! When did you get bigger?"

"Fascinating," said Kopaka, eyeing Takanuva, who was now several inches taller than anyone else in the room. "It's similar to the way the Matoran of Light are taller than any others we have known. Perhaps it's this place, the energies of it, working on their unique systems."

Normally, Onua would have been in the middle of this conversation, but something was nagging at him. He walked slowly around the interior of the Codrex, looking at everything. When he turned back to the group, he sounded mystified and puzzled. "I know this place . . . why do I know this place?"

Now that he had mentioned it, the others felt it, too — a sense that they had stood inside the Codrex before, but no clear memory of when it had been or why. Lewa looked the most uneasy. "I seem to remember fighting here, arguing," he said. "And then . . . it's all a blank."

"Maybe this is the answer," said Kopaka. He was pointing at six empty slots that, from their shape, must have once held large, cylindrical objects. "Just about the right size for Toa canisters, wouldn't you say?"

"You mean . . . ?" began Gali.

"This is the place?" said Pohatu, stunned. "This is where we came from?"

When the Toa had first emerged on the shores of the island of Mata Nui a year before, they had come out of vehicles called Toa canisters. Their memories were largely a blank. They knew instinctively they had been in the canisters a very long time, but they had no idea where they had been before the island they now saw before them. Their pasts had been a mystery. Now part of that mystery had been solved.

"We all felt as if we had seen Karda Nui before," said Kopaka. "Now we know why. At some point in the past, we came here and entered the Codrex. Then we climbed into Toa canisters to wait until we were needed."

Silence fell on the chamber for a few

moments. It was Tahu who finally broke the mood. "We don't have time for memories," he said. "When this is over, maybe we can sort it all out. For now, we have a job to do."

The interior of the Codrex was dominated by complex machinery. Tahu doubted that even a skilled inventor like Nuparu would be able to make sense of any of it. But the keystones had given clear direction on what they had to accomplish here. Onua walked to the bank of machines on the far left and ran his hand across a panel. It flared to life, and as it did so, the Toa Nuva heard a harsh rumble.

Before the startled eyes of the Toa, the section of floor that had once held their canisters began to descend. As it did, it revealed a vast sublevel the heroes had never dreamed existed in the Codrex. Slowly and silently, the segment settled into place far below. The moment it did so, six huge lightstones rose out of its surface, one by where each canister had once rested, forming a circle.

Using their flying abilities, the Toa

descended through the hole to investigate. So caught up were they in this new discovery that none of them realized they had company: Antroz, hidden by his chameleon power and following the sounds of the Toa's voices and movement. He had left Radiak behind, since his ability to disguise his presence would not extend to the Matoran. That left him vulnerable, but right now, he didn't care. He sensed an amazing source of power down below, and he was going to find it.

The chamber was laid out like a huge wheel, with the lightstone ring in the center and three spokes leading off it. The Toa landed on those spokes and then moved in different directions to explore. Pohatu reached the wide end of a spoke first. As soon his armored foot touched a certain plate in the floor, there was a sound of machinery humming. The next instant, Pohatu was looking at a metallic cocoon that had abruptly locked into place beside him, with sound and light coming through cracks in its shell. When it withdrew, it left in its place an impressively large crimson air vehicle, looking as new as if it had been assembled the day before. It was a technological marvel, practically radiating power even while sitting still. It bristled with weaponry and the advanced engine and sleek lines hinted at enormous speed.

Pohatu turned to see that Lewa and Kopaka had made similar discoveries. Of the other two vehicles, one was green and the other blue. Lewa, in particular, was delighted at the find. Tahu was more interested in the ring of lightstones, which had been mentioned in the keystone inscriptions.

"Okay, we may have been here before," said Lewa, smiling. "But we never saw those. I would have ever-remembered."

Gali crouched down and read the inscriptions carved beneath the vehicles. "Axalara T9 . . . Jetrax T6 . . . Rockoh T3. None of those names mean anything to me. How about the rest of you?"

"Why hide things like that in here?" wondered Onua. "Were we supposed to use them somehow?"

"Look at the weapons," marveled Lewa. "Those are for fighting!"

"Could be," agreed Pohatu. "Or maybe escape, if everything goes real wrong."

Kopaka gave a sharp laugh. "If 'everything goes real wrong,' brother, there won't be anywhere to escape to."

With great effort, Icarax had made his way down to the swamp. No doubt by now Toa Ignika had found the Nuva and warned them of the imminent destruction of everything. He wondered how they had reacted. Fear? Hesitation? Or a fierce determination to keep fighting? Probably the last, he decided — Toa were just stupid enough for that.

Down below, he could see Vamprah, Chirox, Gorast, and Bitil surrounding the Codrex. To anyone else, it would have looked like they were putting their all into breaking through the energy field that surrounded the structure. Icarax knew better. They wanted to get in, that was true, but when the time was right, not before.

The Final Battle

Thanks to the grand Plan of Makuta Teridax, the Brotherhood's leader, the proud Makuta had been reduced to timekeepers.

He was surprised to see Krika hovering in the air, not far from the Codrex but not close enough to be part of the effort to break in. Icarax had never particularly liked Krika, seeing him as another Makuta who spent more time thinking than doing. But with the Plan so close to success, Icarax didn't have the luxury of choosing his allies.

"They will never get in there in time, you know," he said as he approached the ghostly figure.

"In time for what?" replied Krika.

"To stop them from waking up Mata Nui, of course," said Icarax. "The Toa are about to undo the only part of this Plan that ever made any sense, while we stand around and do nothing about it."

Krika shot an irritated glance at his companion. Everyone knew Icarax wanted to be leader of the Brotherhood, and achieving that meant proving he had a better plan than the current leader. Unfortunately, Icarax's plans were about as subtle as an axe to the head and only half as interesting. "And what is it you expect to do about it?"

"I expect *us* to act," Icarax snapped. "You know what will happen if the Toa wake up the Great Spirit. There will be no turning back then. We have to strike while his body still sleeps — we have to destroy the Codrex and the Toa with it!"

Krika was tempted to reject the suggestion completely, but he couldn't bring himself to do it. Hadn't he been hovering here, thinking much the same thing? The Toa were inside the structure; it was just a matter of time now. And once the Toa achieved their destiny, well, Great Beings help the world that would result from their actions.

"All right," Krika said. "Speak. I will listen."

Icarax's plan was daring, bold, and naturally, incredibly risky for someone other than him. The energy field around the Codrex had to be brought down. A joint attack by multiple Makuta could do it, but that wasn't going to happen, at least not in time. That was where Krika came in.

The field had been designed by the Great Beings to repel known forces. But Krika's powers were the result of a mutation, something that couldn't be foreseen. As he descended in his ghostly form toward the Codrex, he remembered Icarax's final words.

"I will be surprised if you survive," Icarax had said, his tone suggesting it wouldn't be an altogether pleasant surprise. "But if you do not, at least you are dying in battle. Can anyone ask for more?"

Krika descended as rapidly as he could toward the Codrex. He could see Bitil pointing toward him. If the other Makuta guessed what he was about to do, they would try to stop him. He wasn't going to let that happen. Icarax was right: This was the last chance to prevent disaster.

Steeling himself, he reduced his mass as much as he possibly could. This was the crucial moment. Would the field simply repel him like it did everything else? Or would his form be ghostly enough to pass at least part of the way in?

The tip of his foreleg struck the field . . . and made it through! Krika pushed forward, but each succeeding moment made the going harder. The field was adjusting to block him. It felt like he was trying to swim through thick mud.

When he was about halfway through, all progress was stopped. He knew he was about an instant away from being ejected from the field. The time to act was now. Willing himself to become solid, he materialized in the energy field. The pain was excruciating as the defensive shield threatened to tear him apart. Sparks flew in every direction and the only question was, which would die first — Krika or the field?

"Krika has betrayed us," said Gorast, biting off her words. "He knew when we were to pierce the field. He is trying to sabotage the Plan!"

"Then stop him!" raged Bitil.

She was already in the air with Vamprah

beside her. "It's already too late," Gorast said. "But we can have our revenge."

Inside the Codrex, the Toa felt a jolt of energy as the field disintegrated. "Something's disrupted it," said Onua. "It's going to come down."

"And they're going to come in," added Pohatu.

"Not if we go out there first," said Kopaka, nodding toward the three vehicles.

Lewa smiled. "I like it. I like it."

The disruption and destruction of the field was complete. Unable to eject an object partway through its substance — Krika — the field's energy fed back on itself. The device in the Codrex that had created the protective shield overloaded. With a blinding flash and an explosion of pure force, the field came down.

So did Krika. He fell a long way, too stunned to turn intangible, and so hit the ground hard. He ended up almost completely buried in the mud. When he had shaken himself out of his daze and crawled back to the surface, he expected to see Gorast or one of the other Makuta standing over him, ready to strike. But there was no one there.

A glance upward revealed the reason why. Gorast and Vamprah were closing in on Icarax. Their target hadn't noticed yet, though — he was too busy destroying the Codrex.

FIVE

For the first time since his killing of Botar, that teleporting tool of the Toa, Icarax was having a good time.

He had savored the sight of the energy field collapsing and allowed himself a moment to decide just how best to destroy the Codrex and the Toa inside. With that done, Mata Nui could never be awakened and the great Plan of Makuta Teridax would die a quick death. He finally settled on the direct approach: a surge of gravity to crush the structure and its occupants like a madu fruit.

The metal of the Codrex was already starting to buckle with a most satisfying crunching sound. He could imagine the panicked Toa inside, frantically using their powers to try to stave off doom. That might even work for a while, but eventually the power of a Makuta would be too much for them.

And then, oh, and then, Mata Nui will sleep forever. Makuta Teridax will be blocked, his grand plan in tatters. If the Brotherhood still wishes for universal domination, they will have to do it my way — with thunder and protosteel.

Icarax increased the output of force. He was impatient to see the Codrex flattened and the matter of Teridax's leadership settled once and for all. He would be a just ruler, a fair ruler — only a handful of Makuta would have to die horribly for their loyalty to the fallen Teridax. Mounting their Kanohi masks on poles around the fortress of Destral would serve as a warning to anyone else that might show poor judgment in the future.

And speaking of fools, thought Icarax. He had caught the approach of Vamprah and Gorast out of the corner of his eye. This, he decided, was going to be fun.

While not panicked, the Toa Nuva and Takanuva were certainly worried. The roof and walls above were starting to cave in.

The Final Battle

There was no need to talk. They knew what they had to do. Onua, Pohatu, and Kopaka created pillars of earth, stone, and ice to try to brace the roof. Lewa increased the air pressure along the sides of the chamber in an effort to force the walls back into shape.

"It's not working!" said Pohatu. "We need to think of something else!"

"We have to take the vehicles and get out there," Kopaka said to Tahu. "It's the only way. Maybe we can buy enough time."

Tahu looked into the eyes of the Toa of Ice, with whom he had frequently clashed over the past year. He saw the determination in them and knew he couldn't talk Kopaka out of his plan. "I'll go, too," said the Toa of Fire.

"No," said Kopaka. "If this doesn't work, you will need to think of something else." He turned to the other Toa. "Who wants to go for a ride?"

"I wouldn't miss it," answered Lewa. "If I gave up a chance to fly-ride one of these beauties, Turaga Matau would never forgive me."

"I'll go," offered Pohatu. "I'm no use in here. Besides, this place gives me the creeps."

Lewa was already climbing into the cockpit of the largest craft, the red Axalara T9. "One question. How do we get these things *out* of here?"

"Well, this button says, 'Launch,'" said Pohatu, seated in the Rockoh T3. "Maybe the wall opens or something."

"Then we'd better go while there still is wall," said Kopaka.

Before the question could be debated further, the figure of Antroz suddenly appeared, descending from the upper level. Following the sound of Kopaka's voice and the power radiating from the Jetrax T6 that the Toa of Ice stood near, Antroz headed for the cockpit of that vehicle. He landed at the controls, and the instant he did so, beams of force shot from the console and into his mask. Suddenly, he felt at one with the ship. He could see what its scanners could see, react as fast as the ship's systems could do.

With a shout of triumph, he launched the

Jetrax. It surged forward, brushing against one of the lightstones as it did so. A spark flared, sending energy coursing through the ship and making its armor glow yellow. Then the Jetrax shot straight up through the hole leading to the upper level and right for the solid ceiling. Just as it was about to strike that barrier, the vehicle and its pilot shifted out of phase, becoming ghostly in appearance. The next instant, Antrox and the Jetrax T6 passed unharmed through the ceiling.

Antroz found himself in a bizarre series of metallic tunnels that wound and twisted for an impossible distance. His link to the ship made navigation easy, but he wondered just where these tunnels would lead to. Those questions were cut off by the discovery that Lewa and Pohatu were in pursuit, the Toa of Air in the Axalara T9 and the Toa of Stone in the Rockoh T3. Antroz laughed — they would catch him, all right, but they might not be very glad they did.

Back in the Codrex, there wasn't time to be shocked over what had just happened. The force of gravity still threatened the structure. The pillars created by the Toa were shattering. And they had barely begun the process of awakening Mata Nui. But Takanuva's thoughts were elsewhere.

"I have to go out there," he said quietly.

"We need you here," Gali answered. "If the Makuta should break in —"

"The Makuta need to pay for what they've done!" Takanuva suddenly raged. "Destroying Ta-Koro . . . killing Toa Lhikan, and who knows how many others . . . corrupting innocent Matoran . . . they need to be crushed! And I have the power to do it — with my light energy, I can shred their armor and incinerate their energies!"

It was Tahu who grabbed Takanuva and spun him around. "Listen to yourself!" the Toa of Fire said. "Lost in fury, steeped in violence . . . you sound like a Makuta."

Takanuva shuddered. He knew Tahu was right. Ever since the attack of the shadow leech on Metru Nui, he had been fighting against the dark side of himself. Now it seemed like he was losing.

"All the more reason for me to leave," he said. "What if I lose control in here, with all of you? And there's more . . . I put two and two together, Tahu. I know I had to have been a Matoran of Light once, long before I ever lived on Metru Nui. Otherwise, I couldn't have become a Toa of Light. I don't know what happened or how I was made to forget that, but those are my people out there."

Tahu nodded. He knew he would have said the same thing if there were Matoran of Fire outside the walls of the Codrex.

"If they are out there when that energy storm hits, they are all dead," Takanuva continued. "I won't — I can't — let that happen. I have to find a way to get them out of Karda Nui."

"You'll never make it," said Gali. "The Makuta will destroy you before you're six steps from the Codrex."

"Oh no," said Takanuva, with a grim smile. He held out his hands, one crackling with light energy, the other with shadow.

"Trust me — they've never seen anything like me before."

The three vehicles had emerged from the Codrex into Karda Nui.

"Look out, Brotherhood of Bats and Bugs!" shouted Lewa, knifing through the air in pursuit of Antroz. "Here comes Lewa, king of the sky!"

Lights began to dance in Lewa's eyes. It took him a moment to realize that his mask had changed shape again, and the points of light he saw represented Makuta in flight. His Kanohi now had a built in scanner feature, and that was not good news for his enemies.

Lewa spotted Bitil moving to intercept. The Toa of Air flipped a red lever on the cockpit console. The side panels of the ship dropped down, revealing two Midak Skyblasters. Lewa veered right and dove toward, firing light spheres at the Makuta. Bitil immediately summoned duplicates of himself from his past in an effort to outnumber and overwhelm the Toa.

"Yeah, I heard about that quick-trick you do," Lewa yelled down at the crowd of Bitils. "You know, making doubles of yourself. Go ahead, I won't worry-mind — just gives me more targets!"

As it turned out, Lewa had laughed a little too soon. Half the Bitils unleashed magnetic power that pinned the Axalara in place, while the other used laser vision to start shearing the vehicle's armor off. Lewa's air power was enough to blow some of the Makuta away, but the rest hung on and pressed their attack.

Pohatu saw what was happening. Steering his craft toward the battle, he rammed the Rockoh into the mob of identical Makuta, scattering them like pebbles in a rockslide.

Antroz had slowed the Jetrax to see what had happened to his pursuers. He was so engrossed in the battle that he did not realize until it was too late that Radiak had climbed on board the vehicle.

"What do you want?" Antroz snarled.

"To help," answered Radiak. "To aid you in destroying the Toa Nuva and seeing the great Plan succeed."

Antroz frowned. The process of corrupting these Matoran had worked well, but at times their parroting of trite Brotherhood phrases grew tiresome. "Does it appear I need your help?"

Radiak looked confused. "But . . . but your sight . . . I mean . . . you said we would go into battle together. . . ."

"I no longer need you to be my eyes," said Antroz, hurling him out of the ship. "You're just excess baggage now."

Kopaka, newly emerged from the Codrex, spotted Radiak falling. He knew from Onua what happened to anyone who fell into the waters of the swamp, how they were mutated and twisted by that murk. So he never hesitated, soaring to catch the shadow Matoran before he hit the swamp.

There was a sudden burst of light from the direction of the Codrex. Then Takanuva was flying toward Kopaka, dodging bolts of shadow as he came. The Matoran Photok, Solek, and Tanma were right behind him. "I'll take care of the villager," Takanuva said. "You go after your ship."

"Take care of me?" laughed Radiak darkly. "You can't even take care of yourself! Toa of Light, hah! You look more like a Toa of Twilight to me."

"Shut up, Radiak," Tanma said. "That isn't you talking — it's what the shadow leech did to you."

"And I like it," Radiak said, with a sickening smile.

"Enough," said Takanuva. "This is my job, Kopaka. Go and do yours."

Inside the Codrex, Gali, Onua, and Tahu labored, as Toa Ignika watched, puzzled. What they were trying to achieve was not, in itself, enormously difficult. According to what was inscribed on the keystones, the presence of a Toa would send multiple pulses of energy through the lightstones to awaken Mata Nui. Each one had to be progressively stronger, acting like a jolt to the Great Spirit's system. With luck, they would shock him awake.

There were problems, though. For one thing, there was no telling what would happen to a Toa in the middle of all that. Plus, sending one pulse after another took time, and time was in short supply.

"There has to be a faster way," said Tahu.

Onua nodded. "I've been doing some math. Ignika says when his mask goes from silver to black, we're all doomed. At the rate it's changing, we won't make it in time."

Gali glanced at Tahu. His eyes were narrowed and there was a gleam in them she recognized all too well. It usually meant he was about to suggest something incredibly dangerous and utterly insane.

He didn't disappoint her. "Then we need to do it all at once — one massive jolt."

"That would wake him up," Onua agreed. Then he added, quietly, "Or kill him."

The Final Battle

Gali looked again at the lightstones. "Impossible," she said. "We'll blow up all this and the Codrex and maybe all of Karda Nui."

"If we build up the power through the lightstones, yes," Tahu said. "But what if we had another source? Something so incredible it could feed all the energy we need into this system, all at once?"

"Sure," said Onua. "But where are we going to find something like . . . that . . ." Onua's voice trailed off. He turned to look at Toa Ignika. Tahu and Gali were already doing the same.

"Come here, brother," Tahu said to Ignika. "We need to have a little talk."

SIX

Takanuva held tight to the struggling Radiak as he flew. He had no idea how he was going to get the Matoran out of Karda Nui safely, let alone how he would convince all the shadow Matoran to come. But it hadn't been so very long ago that he was one of them, just a villager doing his job (well, sometimes) and trying to survive in a dangerous world. When the Toa came to the island of Mata Nui, he looked up to them as heroes just as the other villagers did. Now it was time for him to be a hero for these Matoran.

He was so lost in thought that he didn't spot Vican until Photok called out. Takanuva fired a warning burst of light at the flying figure, followed by one of shadow. Vican stopped and hovered in the air.

"Are you . . . are you a Toa?" the Matoran

70

asked. He sounded like someone waking up from a dream. "Yes, you must be. Please, you have to listen to me! Something's happened!"

Takanuva hesitated. This certainly didn't look like a Matoran of Light, or any other kind, not with the wings and claws. "Who are you? What do you want?"

"My name is Vican," the flying figure said. "I was . . . I *am* . . . a Le-Matoran. I worked for Makuta Mutran . . . he was making a Rahi, and it attacked me . . . and now . . . I don't feel like myself. Or rather, I do, but like the old me, not the new me."

"Slow down," snapped Takanuva. "You're not making sense."

"He never did," grumbled Radiak.

"I hate to agree with Radiak," said Solek. "But I wouldn't trust him. He's one of them."

"No! Mutran used a shadow leech on me, before we came here," Vican explained, talking so fast his words tumbled over each other. "It changed me, how I felt, how I looked at the world. All I cared about was darkness and destruction . . . the things I helped Mutran do and create . . . Mata Nui forgive me."

For a moment, Vican was too choked with emotion to go on. When he had recovered himself, he continued. "After the Rahi attack, suddenly I realized how far into the darkness I fell. I saw myself for what I became and it made me sick. But I'm not that twisted thing anymore — I'm not! You have to believe me."

Radiak chuckled. "Nice one. I'll have to remember this trick after I get free from ol' Twilight here."

"It's no trick!" insisted Vican.

"We've seen this before," said Tanma. "Shadow Matoran coming back, playing on our feelings, trying to win our trust so they can trap us. I know what to do with his kind. Let me —"

Takanuva made a sharp gesture to cut Tanma off. He was remembering how a shadow leech attacked him on Metru Nui, leaving him half in light, half in shadow. If what this Vican was saying was true, then there might be a way to undo what the leech did, not only for himself but for the shadow Matoran as well.

"Where is this Rahi now?" Takanuva asked.

"Don't tell me you believe him?" said Photok.

"Answer the question," Takanuva persisted.

"It flew off to the east, then headed up to the clouds," Vican replied. "I was chasing it."

"All right," said the Toa. "Now *we* are chasing it."

Icarax couldn't help but laugh. Only two Makuta dispatched to stop him, and one of them blinded and relying on a Matoran to be his eyes? If he wasn't so amused, he would have been insulted.

Vamprah was no problem, of course. Icarax hurled a bolt of shadow energy to the Makuta's left. When Vamprah veered right to dodge, he moved right into the path of a blast of laser vision. It hit its target — not Vamprah, but Gavla. She toppled off the Makuta's back.

Icarax smiled at Vamprah's reaction. The

bat-like Makuta had been blinded days ago. He was able to see thanks to a telepathic link with Gavla, activated whenever the two were in physical contact. With Gavla now falling to her death, Vamprah was truly blind.

"The great hunter," Icarax said with a sneer. "Terror of the Matoran. What are you now? Nothing but prey."

Vamprah hurled a sonic blast in the direction of Icarax's voice. The energy knocked Icarax back, but did no real damage.

"So the bat has fangs, does it?" Icarax said. "When I run the Brotherhood, we will have to see about pulling them."

"You will never lead!" The harsh words came from an angry Gorast. She had rescued Gavla and deposited the shadow Matoran on a mud bank. Now she was ready to settle things with Icarax.

"Stop and think," said Icarax. "My way offers much more opportunity for battle than our current leader's ever can. Join with me!"

"Never!" screamed Gorast, slashing with

her wing blades. Her blow tore open part of Icarax's chest plate. She flashed a look of evil triumph. Any moment now, she knew, the energy of which all Makuta are made would come seeping out of the gash and the battle would be won.

To her shock, nothing happened. Icarax clutched the wound in his armor and smiled bitterly. "Did I forget to tell you? I ran into Toa Ignika. In an effort to defeat me, he changed me from pure energy back to a true bio-mechanical being, muscle and tissue connected to armor. So I can't be beaten just by cutting a gap in my shell and letting my essence leak out."

Icarax's multi-bladed sword began to rotate faster and faster, as he said, "Too bad, Gorast, that the same can't be said of you."

Divide and conquer, Pohatu thought as he piloted the Rockoh through a tight turn.

The Makuta forces had split up. Gorast and Vamprah had gone after Icarax; Krika had vanished; Mutran, too, was nowhere in sight; and as soon as he spotted Takanuva, Antroz had sent Bitil and Chirox after him. That left Antroz alone against Lewa, Pohatu, and Kopaka.

Not that the Makuta seemed to mind. In full control of the Jetrax T6, he had darted around, over and through every obstacle Pohatu or Lewa had thrown in his way, and outpaced Kopaka with ease. Hitting and running, he had already done significant damage to the Rockoh.

Now Lewa was on Antroz's tail in the Axalara T9. The Toa of Air was buffeting Antroz's ship with gale-force winds in an effort to crash it into the forest of stone pillars created by Pohatu. Earlier, Antroz had used his magnetic power to send the Axalara into a spin, and only quick action by Lewa had kept it from crashing into the swamp.

Antroz spotted the Rockoh and fired. The Jetrax's skyblasters hit their target, sending the Rockoh into a spin. Pohatu fought to right the ship, but it was headed for one of the stone pillars he had created. Quickly, he used his elemental power to shatter the rock before the ship collided with it.

Lewa banked to the left, trying to flank Antroz. The Axalara was a more powerful ship, but the Jetrax was faster. He needed to box Antroz in somehow.

Further behind, Kopaka had been working at the same thing. But every ice wall he threw up got blown to pieces by the Jetrax's weapons or smashed by the vehicle itself. Every rain of hailstones had been shrugged off by Antroz and bounced harmlessly off the Jetrax's armored hull.

Pohatu was back in the fight now, and he was angry. Timing it just right, he made a hand of stone erupt out of the swamp and grab the Jetrax. Before Antroz could power it free, Pohatu hit the controls and pulled the Rockoh's wings in for a dive. Firing as he flew, he raked the side of the Jetrax with bolts of energy.

Antroz jolted the craft free of the stone hand and wheeled in midair, firing at the Rockoh.

When Pohatu dodged, Antroz used his gravity power to send the Toa's ship plunging toward the swamp.

Lewa closed in, rocking the Jetrax with fire from the Axalara's skyblasters and shattering the Makuta's concentration. Free of the increased pull of gravity, Pohatu managed to right his ship just as it skimmed the surface of the water.

Then it was Kopaka's turn. He used his power to drop the temperature around the Jetrax hundreds of degrees in an instant, slowing down the vehicle's engines and cutting its speed. Lewa and Pohatu closed in from both sides, ready to destroy the wounded craft.

Only Kopaka was close enough to see what happened next. Just as the two Toa vessels came in range, Antroz disappeared from the cockpit using his power to teleport. Acting quickly, Kopaka threw up ice barriers in front of the Axalara and the Rockoh, shouting, "Stop!"

Neither craft could turn in time, smashing

into and through the ice. But the barriers had delayed them just long enough for Kopaka to climb behind the controls of the Jetrax. "All right," said the Toa of Ice. "If this is the final battle, let's make it one to remember."

Tahu's heartlight was flashing wildly. His breath was coming in ragged gasps. Pinned against the wall by Toa Ignika, he knew he was about to die from an overdose of the power of Life.

The Toa of Fire had been trying to explain his plan. Using the Mask of Life, the Toa would try to accomplish all at once what it would otherwise take hours to do. The mask's power, delivered in one great jolt, would awaken Mata Nui abruptly. Tahu couldn't be sure it would work, because the mask might not be able to feed into the lightstones. But the only way to find out would be for the Ignika to give up its body and its attempts to be a real living being, and go back to being just a mask.

Toa Ignika hadn't taken this well.

Onua and Gali had rushed up and were

trying to pull Ignika away from Tahu. "Let go!" yelled Onua. "You're killing him!"

Tahu had no choice. Summoning his control of heat and flame, he drove the temperature of his armor up 1,000 degrees in a split second. Crying out in pain, Ignika let go. Tahu staggered, trying to catch his breath.

"That's . . . that's the problem with being alive," the Toa of Fire said. "You can feel pain. You can die. Just like everyone in this universe is going to die if we don't awaken Mata Nui and bring balance back to the universe. We need you to do that!"

Ignika flung Onua and Gali off of him with such force they slammed against the walls. He began to advance on Tahu again. Bracing for the attack, flames crackled around Tahu's hands.

Gali got to her feet and got in between the two. "Ignika, stop and think! Think! Why did you want to become a Toa? Why did you want to become like us? There had to be a reason!"

Toa Ignika stopped in midstride and

frowned. Searching his memory, he came up with a name. "Matoro . . ."

Gali glanced at Onua, who nodded. "That's right, Ignika, Matoro," she said. "We know he died a hero. He sacrificed everything so a universe could live. And if he inspired you to be a hero too, then can you do less than he? If Matoro were here in your place, what do you think his answer would be?"

There was a long moment of silence. Each of the Toa waited, their eyes searching Ignika's features for some sign of what his answer would be. This one single instant would decide the fate of an entire universe and all its people.

"He would say . . ." Ignika began. "He would say yes."

Toa Ignika stood straight and looked at Tahu. Gesturing toward the mask he wore, Ignika said, "I will do what must be done. Then I will be like Matoro. I will be a hero."

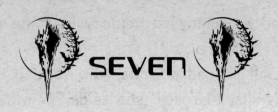

SEVEN

Mutran was growing impatient. He had sent Vican off after the klakk a long time ago, and he had not returned, nor had the escaped Rahi. There was no excuse for this. Maybe it was time he gave Vican a few extra wings and maybe a tentacle or two, to teach him to focus on his job.

His grumbling ceased at the sight of Antroz materializing in front of him. The crimson-armored Makuta had made several short teleports to reach this part of the swamp and his fatigue showed.

"It's time," said Antroz. "We have to be prepared."

Mutran furled and unfurled his small wings, a sure sign he was uneasy. He dropped his voice to a whisper and said, "Is this really wise, letting them wake up the Great Spirit? What if he remembers who put him to sleep in the first place?"

Antroz shot a fierce look at Mutran. "You know the Plan. You agreed to it and profited from it and you *will* carry it out. Our orders were clear: delay the Toa Nuva until the appointed hour; allow them to awaken Mata Nui; and then eliminate them as a threat. Only they could revive the Great Spirit, so they had to remain alive to do so — but we don't need to suffer their presence one moment past that."

"All right," said Mutran. "What do you want me to do?"

"Find Radiak or another shadow Matoran so my sight can be restored. Then go help Gorast against Icarax. If he kills the Toa Nuva before they carry out their mission, The Plan is doomed."

Mutran nodded and took to the air to carry out his new instructions. But knowing Antroz could not see him, he did not fly very fast. He saw no reason to fly headlong into the blades of Icarax.

*   *   *

Gorast could have used the help. Icarax's strategy was as simple as it was deadly: Slash open her armor and then use laser vision to incinerate her energy as it leaked out. The success of this method had forced her to keep her distance from Icarax and left Vamprah alone in the fight.

But now she had a plan of her own. In combat, Icarax had no equal, but his love of battle could also be a weakness. Gorast knew this well, for it was a weakness she shared. Still, for her scheme to work, she needed a distraction.

That was when she spotted Mutran, far off to the west. He was dispatching a shadow Matoran on some unknown mission, and when that was done, he glanced toward where Vamprah and Icarax were fighting. He looked about as eager to join that battle as a Matoran of Stone is to join a group swim.

Too bad the fool doesn't have a choice, Gorast said to herself as she shot toward him. Before Mutran could protest, she was dragging him toward the scene of the clash.

"I need you to send your thoughts into Icarax's mind," she hissed. "Any thoughts. Screams. Babble. Anything so that he does not pick up on what I am sending to Vamprah."

Mutran nodded. That seemed relatively safe — safer, at any rate, than saying no to an enraged Gorast.

"Then do it now."

Mutran sent a telepathic wave of white noise at Icarax. As he did so, Gorast sent a mental message of her own to Vamprah. Once she was sure it had been received, she moved in to attack.

Gavla had made her way back to Vamprah's back, so the Makuta could see once more. He darted and dodged, staying out of reach of Icarax's blades and parrying his blasts of laser vision and his hurled lightning. This gave Gorast the chance to swoop in behind Icarax and land a crushing blow with two of her four arms.

As Icarax whirled to face this new opponent, Gorast backed off, laughing. "No need to worry, Vamprah," she said. "Mutran brings a message from below. The Toa Nuva are about to awaken Mata Nui. The Plan will succeed!"

She knew how Icarax would react. All his hopes of someday leading the Brotherhood of Makuta depended on showing he had a better plan than the one they were following — and that meant the current plan had to fail. He couldn't allow the Toa Nuva to achieve their destiny.

Vamprah and Gorast blocked him from the Codrex. But he was a Makuta, with all the power that came with it. He would not be prevented from the battle he craved with the Toa, the battle he knew he had to fight if his dreams of conquest were to ever come true.

"I will deal with you later," he growled, his body shimmering as he began to teleport away.

"Now!" screamed Gorast, grabbing Icarax and triggering her ability to make his power run wild.

Vamprah unleashed a burst of energy. Even as the act of teleporting transformed Icarax's body into scattered atoms, Vamprah's attack disrupted those atoms. The combination of the two plus Gorast's attack was devastating. The sparkling molecules of Icarax's body shot off in a million different directions. Icarax's scream went from earsplitting to a mere ghostly echo in a split second.

Mutran stared at the empty space that Icarax had once occupied. "What just happened?" he asked. "And that was repulsive — so how could we make it happen again?"

"When you teleport, your atoms are scattered and then drawn back together at your destination," Gorast answered. "By increasing his power and then disrupting them at the crucial moment, they flew all over the known universe in an instant."

"So Icarax will never finish his teleport?"

"Oh, he will finish," Gorast smiled. "Part of him will finish in Karda Nui ... and part in Destral ... and part in Metru Nui ... and part in the southern islands ... and other parts in a thousand other places. You get the idea."

Mutran returned her smile. Icarax had always wanted to be a presence throughout the

universe. This method of achieving it was probably not quite what he'd had in mind.

Takanuva, with the three Matoran of Light and
Radiak in tow, had climbed through the sky to
the Matoran villages. So far, it had been a frus-
trating search for this Rahi that Vican claimed
was called a "klakk." The one thing everyone
agreed on was that klakk was a really odd name.

It was Radiak who spotted it first. If he
hadn't said or done anything, the others might
have missed it completely. But instead he fired a
shadow bolt in the klakk's direction, which went
wide. The near miss was enough to anger the
flying Rahi, which circled back and screamed
at the shadow Matoran.

Takanuva was bracing to cut off another
attack by Radiak. It turned out that wouldn't be
necessary. Radiak blinked, shook his head, and
dropped his hands to his sides. This time, when
he struggled to get free of Takanuva's grasp, the
Toa of Light let him go. Photok and Tanma immediately protested, but Takanuva cut them off.

Radiak made no effort to escape. Instead, he looked around at the three Matoran of Light as if they were long-lost friends — which, of course they were. "Are you...all right? I didn't...hurt anyone...did I?"

"Oh, please," Tanma said, disgusted that anyone was buying this obvious act.

"Tanma, wait a second," Solek said. "Radiak, do you remember what happened to you?"

Radiak nodded, eyes downcast. "I fought you...I tried to kill you."

"Radiak," said Photok. "If you're really back on our side — what are the Makuta planning?"

"I overheard Antroz talking once. He said the Makuta wanted the Toa to wake up Mata Nui, but he didn't say why. Then, once the Great Spirit was awake, they...we...would kill the Toa and corrupt any Matoran of Light who were left."

Takanuva pondered. Radiak's transformation seemed incredible, but there had to be an explanation for it. Perhaps whatever the shadow leeches did to drain light from their victims also created some kind of barrier to prevent light from returning later. The sonic tones of the klakk's attack somehow shattered that barrier. With the return of light to the being, the corruption of the Makuta faded away.

But if Radiak was telling the truth — how could the Makuta possibly benefit from Mata Nui waking up? If they wanted him awake, why put him to sleep 1,000 years ago in the first place? And if his awakening was part of their plan, what did that mean? Did the Toa Nuva have to abandon fulfilling their destiny?

"Find the rest of the shadow Matoran," he said to his four companions. "Get them here. We're going to keep this Rahi good and angry, and cure all the rest of them. And then we're getting all the Matoran out of this place."

"What?" said Tanma. "You mean we're going to give it up to the Makuta? No way! This is our home and we'll fight for it."

"Listen to me!" said Takanuva, grabbing Tanma by the shoulders and resisting the urge to shake some sense into the Matoran. The anger in his tone shocked the others to silence. "No one is going to be fighting for anything. If Mata Nui awakens, this whole place — all of Karda Nui — is going to be caught in the biggest energy storm you can imagine. Nothing will survive it. And that's why I am getting every Matoran out of here, even if I have to drag you!"

So wrapped up were Takanuva and the Matoran in the argument that none of them noticed the ghostly form of Makuta Krika hovering nearby. At the news that all of Karda Nui would be engulfed in a lethal storm as soon as the Great Spirit was awakened, a grim smile came to Krika's mouth.

Very neat indeed, he thought. *Makuta Teridax sends his top lieutenants to Karda Nui to make sure all goes according to the Plan. But he neglects to inform us that our "success" here will end with us all dead. In one move, he achieves his ambitions and eliminates his potential rivals.*

Krika made a decision. Despite the risk — he had, after all, allied with Icarax against the Plan — he had to tell the other Makuta what he had learned. Teridax was betraying them all and had to be stopped.

Krika flew down toward the swamp, desperately trying to think of a way to convince his fellow Makuta that their greatest enemy was their leader.

Two of those Makuta were much closer than Krika thought. Chirox and Bitil had followed Takanuva and the Matoran. Now that all four of the Toa's Matoran companions had scattered, the time had come to attack.

Chirox struck first, using his mask power to make it impossible for Takanuva to hear their approach or call for help. Then it was Bitil's turn, using his mask to summon half a dozen other versions of himself from the past. Against eight Makuta, Takanuva wouldn't have a chance.

The attack began with a hail of shadow bolts, which struck Takanuva from behind. Under ordinary circumstances, that would have been enough to kill him. But since being partially corrupted by a shadow leech and drained of some of his light power, his resistance to shadow had increased. He turned to face his attackers.

Since losing a portion of his light, Takanuva had struggled against the dark impulses that filled him. He was quicker to anger and had to resist the urge to strike out violently at obstacles in his way. But the sight of a horde of Makuta coming toward him stripped away the last of his self-control. Screaming soundlessly, he unleashed a barrage of light bolts.

The Makuta scattered, but continued to advance. Three of the Bitil doubles were trying to circle around behind him. Takanuva responded with lasers that sliced their protosteel weapons to pieces. Then he wheeled and hurled a flare right at Kirop, the Matoran who rode atop Chirox and served as the Makuta's eyes. The sudden flash temporarily blinded the shadow Matoran, and the resulting loss of sight broke Chirox's concentration. Takanuva could hear and speak again.

"Come on, then," the Toa of Light growled.

"Come on! This won't be some kolhii match passing for a battle — any Makuta who gets near me dies!"

Chirox laughed. "You would be violating your code, Toa. Don't you know your kind never kills?"

Takanuva's response was a light bolt that punched a small hole in Chirox's armor. Immediately, the green-black energy that made up a Makuta's substance began to leak out through the gap.

"But I'm not my 'kind,' not anymore — your shadow leeches saw to that," said Takanuva. "I'm half Toa of Light, half Toa of Shadow. This was what you wanted, wasn't it? Toa consumed by darkness, Toa not hampered by things like mercy or morality. Well, now you can choke on it."

Takanuva rocketed forward, blasting light and shadow as he went. If he had been in his right mind, he would have realized charging into a mob of Makuta was suicide. But all he felt was his rage and all he knew was these beings were his enemies, and his enemies had to be destroyed.

The Makuta had other ideas. One of the Bitils had managed to get above and behind Takanuva, and was raising his blade for a fatal strike. Then a blast of light from an unexpected direction knocked the weapon from his hand.

"You look like you could use a hand, brother," shouted Kopaka, piloting the Jetrax T6. Wisps of light energy were still curling from the vehicle's skyblasters.

Takanuva ignored him. He was fighting like a lunatic, tearing his way through Makuta too startled to react. There was no strategy or plan behind his attack, just sheer, brute force and unleashed rage. It was Kopaka who recalled what Toa Onua had said about Bitil's mask power. Targeting the one Bitil who was hanging back from the fight, Kopaka hit him with a skyblaster bolt. Startled, Bitil lost control of his mask power and his doubles vanished from view.

Again, Takanuva didn't notice. He was

bombarding Chirox with light bolts, too fast for the Makuta to be able to staunch the leak of his energy from his armor. Then the Toa of Light tore Kirop off Chirox's back and hurled the Matoran down toward the swamp!

Kopaka had seen enough. He swooped down in the Jetrax and caught Kirop before racing back to Takanuva. Trapping Kirop in ice bonds and setting the vehicle to hover, Kopaka leapt out into space and grabbed Takanuva.

"Toa! Stop this, now!" he shouted. "Remember who you are!"

"I know who I am!" Takanuva replied savagely. "I am what *they* made me!"

"Then you're letting them win, brother," Kopaka said, forcing his voice to be calm. "You're admitting you are no better than they are."

Slowly, reluctantly, Takanuva forced his violent emotions down. Seeing an opening, Bitil unleashed chain lightning, striking both Toa. By the time they recovered and looked around, Bitil and Chirox were gone.

The Final Battle

"This makes no sense," said Kopaka. "He had us right where he wanted us. Even with Chirox wounded, why flee?"

"Because," answered Takanuva. "They know the Toa Nuva are destined to awaken Mata Nui — but they don't know which of you are needed to do it. Kill the wrong one and their whole Plan goes out like a light."

"Their Plan depends on us?" asked Kopaka, in disbelief.

"It's a long story," said Takanuva. "And I better tell it to you — because whatever's going to happen, it's going to happen soon."

NINE

Tahu, Ignika, and Gali stood alone in the Codrex. Onua had left a short time ago to join the fight. Now they stood, poised to do what they had been created to do.

"This is it," said the Toa of Fire. "All the battles we've had, all the adventures, all the danger and death . . . all for this moment."

"It's hard to believe," Gali agreed. "You know, there were so many times when I hated you — when it seemed like you were being stubborn just for its own sake. But now I realize that you were just trying to do your best. It couldn't have been easy leading this group."

Tahu Nuva looked away from the one who was perhaps his dearest friend on the team. For a long time, he didn't say anything. Then he turned back to Gali.

"Do what we set out to do. If the worst

happens, maybe, somehow, you'll be safe in here. Maybe the Codrex can protect you from the storm."

"What? Why?" asked Gali.

"Because I remember now, sister . . . I remember everything that happened," said Tahu, his voice heavy with grief. "Seeing this place again awoke the memories. We were here before."

"I know that," said Gali. "We all felt some recognition of Karda Nui when we first arrived. That doesn't explain —"

"No, I mean we were in the Codrex before," he said. "Pohatu and Kopaka were right — our Toa canisters were housed here and launched from here. I led us into this structure 100,000 years ago, knowing they would be here, knowing that we might never leave again."

He related the story to her as quickly and simply as he could. How he had learned during his team's initial training what their true mission was and what it would involve; how he knew about the energy storm that would hit Karda Nui back then, and purposely delayed so that the Toa would be trapped in the Codrex by it; how he gave them a choice — climb into the canisters to sleep and wait for the time they were needed, or perish in the storm. The only thing he left out was that, at the time, Kopaka had known all this as well. But the Toa of Ice no longer remembered, and he saw no reason to damage Gali's regard for Kopaka by telling her about it.

When he was done, Gali did something he never would have expected: She smiled. "No wonder you didn't want to talk about it when Pohatu brought up the empty canister slots. Tahu, I can't say I am okay with how you did what you did — but I understand why you did it. You had to make a hard decision, but if you hadn't made it, we might not be here now. There might be no one to awaken Mata Nui."

"Thank you," said Tahu. "I should have known if anyone would understand . . ." His voice trailed off. "But I still need to go. My place is out there, fighting this battle, leading my team."

"It would take the Great Beings themselves to keep you away from a fight, I know," Gali said, laying a hand on his arm. "But, listen to me. We will make it out of here. We will win this day, and then someday we will look back on it and wonder how we survived." She laughed. "After all, with Lewa Nuva as a fighter pilot, how can we fail?"

Tahu didn't answer. His thoughts suddenly seemed to be elsewhere. When he returned his attention to Gali, he was smiling. "That's it. The vehicles, like the one Lewa is piloting — that's how we can get out of here in time."

"I don't understand."

"Remember how fast they are, how they passed right through the ceiling when they launched? If they can do that, they can carry us out of Karda Nui in the seconds we'll have before the storm erupts full-force."

Tahu nodded toward Toa Ignika then looked at Gali. "Give me three minutes, and then go ahead. We're going to get home, Gali, all of us. I promise."

Before she could respond, he was out of the Codrex. She began counting down to the moment when the destiny of the Toa Nuva would finally be achieved.

It wasn't hard to get the shadow Matoran to chase the Matoran of Light back up to the sky. Hunting their former friends was, after all, what shadow Matoran loved to do.

Running into an angry klakk, however, was not part of their plans. Feeling threatened, the Rahi attacked anyone who came near and its sonic scream shattered the barrier that kept light from reaching the corrupted Matoran. One by one, they dropped out of the fight as the Makuta's hold on them dwindled away. Finally, only one Matoran remained in the grip of darkness. That was Gavla, the first to fall to a shadow leech when the Makuta invaded Karda Nui.

"Can you lead the Matoran out of here?" Takanuva asked Tanma.

"I think so," Tanma answered. "Vican says there's a portal to the outside in the western wall — he went through it to find Icarax. Of course, there's a Makuta base on the other side, but if we move fast enough —"

"Good," said the Toa of Light. "I'm going after Gavla. When you get out, take the Matoran north, to Metru Nui. There are Toa there, so the place should be well-defended."

After giving Tanma directions as best he could to the island city, Takanuva said good-bye. He headed back for the swamp, in search of the only Matoran left to be rescued. He found her wandering along the shore of a mud islet, not far away from where Vamprah stood with Chirox. Takanuva flew faster than he ever had before and grabbed her, carrying her up to the sky.

As he knew she would, Gavla fought all the way. Takanuva ignored her screams and rants, knowing that in the end she would be happy to be free of the taint of shadow. Sighting the klakk, Takanuva fired a bolt of shadow at it to bait the creature.

The klakk responded as it had each time so far, with a sonic scream, this time targeted at both

Takanuva and Gavla. The Toa of Light immediately felt something change inside him, as light returned to fill the void now occupied in his spirit by darkness. It would take a while, he was sure, before his armor changed back to white and gold from white and gray — but at least he knew the damage done by the shadow leech was being reversed.

Gavla's reaction was quite different. She howled with rage even after the klakk's attack had undone what the shadow leech had done to her. When Takanuva moved to see what was wrong, she struck out at him with a bolt of light.

"Who asked you to save me?" she raged. "Don't you understand? The Makuta accepted me — they had use for me — which is more than my fellow Matoran ever did! I finally found a place where I belonged, and you took it away from me."

"But . . . but you were evil," Takanuva said. "You were threatening people who had been your friends for years."

"Friends?" Gavla said bitterly. "They were never my friends. But you wouldn't understand — you're a Toa. Every Toa is your brother or your sister. You all rush around thinking whatever you do must be right. Well, sometimes it's not."

Takanuva saw it was useless to argue. He wasn't sure how to feel about what she'd said, angry or just sad. "Tanma is gathering the Matoran at the old village to take all of you out of Karda Nui while there's still time. You had better go if you want to join them."

Gavla gave him a long look, her eyes full of sadness and resignation. "I guess I will have to," she said, as she flew past him. "You've left me nowhere else to go."

Down below, the battle was raging more fiercely than before. Gorast, Bitil, and Mutran, with what limited assistance Antroz, Chirox, and Vamprah could provide, were trading bolts and blows with the Toa Nuva. Makuta resistance had stiffened, as they tried to force the Toa back toward the Codrex. Gorast's strategy was simple: pen the Toa into a small area so they would be easy to destroy once Mata Nui was awakened.

Tahu and Gorast were locked in a fight, the Toa using his rotating blade to try and keep her at bay. He knew from Pohatu what would happen if she touched him — loss of control of his elemental powers. If that happened when he was near his allies, he might incinerate all of them.

"The final moments have arrived," Gorast said. "Soon, it will be too late for anyone to change the course of events. The Plan will succeed, and the world as you know it will be history."

"I've heard words like that from Makuta before," Tahu shot back. "They were wrong then, too. Where is the leader of the Brotherhood, by the way? Too cowardly to face us?"

Gorast hissed as a fire bolt scorched her armor. "Do not worry, Toa — you will hear from him soon enough, in words like thunder."

Tahu parried Gorast's blow, but left himself

open to a sonic attack that cracked his adaptive armor. "You fool, no one is going to hear anything if we don't get out of here! When Mata Nui awakes, an energy storm will kill anyone who's still here."

"He's telling the truth!" It was Krika, flying toward them. "I heard the Toa talking up above. Makuta Teridax has set us all up to be killed!"

Krika had done many things in his life, most of them evil, some bordering on insane. But if he had thought Gorast would ever listen to him, that was truly madness. She turned on him with hatred in her eyes, Tahu totally forgotten now, and charged. Before Krika could stop her, she had grabbed his arm and triggered her Mask of Disruption.

"Gorast, no! Don't you understand? You're all doomed!" Krika yelled as he felt his powers slipping out of his control.

"I only understand that you are a traitor," she replied. "And there is only one punishment for traitors!"

Krika screamed then, as his ability to reduce

his mass to intangibility ran wild. With his will no longer able to control his power, he grew more ghostly as his atoms became less and less substantial. Finally, with a cry of pure anguish, he vanished completely from view.

"Gone," Gorast said, satisfied. "Less than a phantom, now, and soon not even that."

Tahu fired his blaster, forming a clamp that pinned Gorast's arms to her sides. Before she could break free, he used his elemental powers to increase the temperature around her until her armor began to soften.

"I ought to let you melt," Tahu said. "How long would your energy survive here, with no body to possess? Krika was trying to save your miserable life, and you repaid him with death."

"Tahu!" Kopaka shouted. "We need to get back to the Codrex. The Makuta want us to wake up Mata Nui — at least, that's what Kirop says. Could this all be some trick?"

Gorast began to laugh. It started out as a soft giggle, then grew into insane peals of mirth that chilled Tahu's spirit. "It's too late, too late," she cried. "Can't you feel it? It has begun — the Great Spirit awakes!"

It was true. The air in Karda Nui had begun to sizzle with energy. Everywhere Tahu looked, the light was growing brighter, dispelling the shadows of the Makuta. In the distance, he could see the Matoran of Light speeding toward the west and, hopefully, safety.

"She's mad," said Tahu. "They all are. The Makuta have been fighting us every step of the way, and now I'm supposed to believe they wanted us to succeed all along? They have a funny way of showing it!"

"What if we're missing something?" asked Kopaka.

"Look around you," said Tahu. "You know what's about to happen. We'll have to worry about 'what if's' later."

Kopaka glanced at the still laughing Gorast, who was clearly either caught up in a feeling of triumph or completely insane. "Let's hope there is a 'later,' then."

*　　*　　*

Toa Ignika rose slowly, majestically, into the air, then descended into the center of the ring of lightstones. For an instant, nothing happened. Then energy lanced from the mask into the six crystals. Toa Ignika staggered as his body began to sparkle, each point of light scattering in a different direction. In a matter of seconds, the body had returned to the random assortment of molecules it had been before the Mask of Life created it. And then it was done, leaving only the mask hovering in the air, trapped in a nimbus of overwhelming power.

A whip of energy suddenly lashed out at Gali. But it caused no pain — instead, it was raw emotion that it carried. At first, she felt a great emptiness. Then there was the sensation of a great mind embracing awareness, reaching out to feel and experience all there was in the universe. She felt joy, a sense of triumph, even a desire for vengeance on the entity's enemies, and something more . . . something indistinct and far away, which she could not quite identify. Perhaps the consciousness was just so powerful, so alien, that it was beyond her ability to understand. She hoped that was all it was.

Then there was another strange happening. The mask itself began to vibrate violently. Power was no longer flowing only from the Kanohi Ignika into the lightstones, but now something was flowing back into the mask! Worried that the energies unleashed might destroy the mask, Gali reached out to tear it free. As soon as she made contact, there was an explosion of force, and she was slammed into the wall.

When she regained consciousness minutes later, it was to see Onua standing over her. "Gali, we have to go. It may already be too late!"

"But the mask . . ." she began.

Onua glanced at the Ignika, which was vibrating so fast now it was just a blur. "There's no time. Life here is coming to an end, and if we don't leave, we'll end with it."

The storm, as most storms do, had started out small. First, the glow beneath the swamp had grown painfully bright. Then a tiny vortex of energy sprang to life just above the murky water. It rapidly grew bigger and bigger, bolts of power flying from it in all directions. Now it was spreading out across the swamp and stabbing upwards toward the sky.

Although the Toa Nuva had been expecting it, the Makuta were the ones who noticed it first. Unable to see, Antrox, Chirox, and Vamprah could only feel the power crackling in the air. Gorast had managed to free herself from the Toa and greeted the storm as if it were a sign of final victory. Bitil was not so sure, and had Gorast not been looking, he would have been winging his way out of Karda Nui.

Mutran was the most curious about the new arrival. Had Vican been around, he would have sent the Matoran into the eye of the storm to check it out. Since he was gone, along with the rest of the Matoran, Mutran steeled himself to check it out on his own. True, it looked dangerous, but it was raw power — if he could tap it, feed it into his creations, who knew what amazing Rahi he might create?

Tentatively, he flew along the very edges of the storm. Yes, it was everything he imagined it to be. The energy was devouring everything in its path: water, stalactites, Rahi beasts . . . everything. But there had to be a way to harness it. He was a Makuta, after all, no mere whirlwind of power was too much for him to master.

Then he saw it — the answer! "It's so absurdly simple," he shouted. "I can control this storm! All I have to do is —"

A crimson bolt of power erupted from the heart of the storm. In a flash, it had disintegrated Mutran's protosteel armor and vaporized the energy being within. In a microsecond, a 100,000 year-old Makuta was gone, leaving not even a cloud of dust to mark his passing.

Now even Gorast realized something was very wrong. The storm was growing in size and strength at blinding speed. "No," she whispered. "It isn't possible. . . ."

"What is it?" demanded Antroz. "What's going on?"

"We have to get away," said Bitil. "Curse us for fools, we've been betrayed!"

"Krika was right. Krika was right," Gorast kept muttering.

"Lead us out of here," Antroz ordered Bitil. But that Makuta shook his head.

"You, Vamprah, and Chirox would only slow me down," Bitil replied, already in flight. "Find your own way home."

Antroz cursed Bitil as he flew away, while Chirox sought out Gorast. But the female Makuta was making no effort to escape. She was simply standing on the shore of the swamp, transfixed by the storm — whether it was the sheer destructive beauty of it, or the elegance of the betrayal it represented, not even she could say. Perhaps it was simply the realization that her leader, Makuta Teridax, had sent her and the others to this place knowing that if their mission was successful, this storm would erupt and slay them all . . . perhaps it was facing that truth that drove her mad.

Bitil would try to teleport to escape the onrushing storm, but it was already too close. Waves of energy interfered with his power and he went nowhere. He pushed his flight ability to its limit, but could not outrace the vortex. And, as Pohatu Nuva once observed, the one power no Makuta had was superspeed.

The Toa Nuva and Takanuva had climbed aboard the three vehicles. Their only hope of escape was that the flying craft could somehow outdistance the storm that signaled Mata Nui's rising.

"Go!" shouted Tahu, and the three rocketed toward the western wall. Karda Nui and the storm that consumed it became a blur as they flew, three in the cockpits, the rest clinging for dear life. Pohatu spotted what he thought was the Mask of Life flying through the air . . . but then it was gone, and he had to wonder if it had ever been there at all. One sight he was certain of was that of the Makuta, fleeing before the storm and doomed to fail in their effort to escape.

"Tahu, the Makuta," shouted Pohatu. "They won't make it! Should we . . . ?"

The Toa Nuva of Fire considered for a split second. It was against the code of a Toa to knowingly kill an enemy or allow one to die if it could be prevented. But he knew in his heart that there was no way to save the Makuta now, and trying would only mean the loss of his team.

"They lit this inferno," he replied. "Let them burn in it."

The vehicles were going beyond fast now and still picking up speed. They were heading for the portal in the western wall through which the Matoran of Light had escaped. But just as the vehicles approached it, a wave of energy rocked them. Suddenly, the Toa were headed for a solid wall.

"Hang on!" Lewa shouted.

The Axalara, Jetrax, and Rockoh shimmered

out of existence, along with the Toa, just long enough to pass unharmed through the walls. The next moment, the Toa were racing through the darkness and hoping to find the light.

Behind them, the storm had grown to its maximum. The Makuta, the Matoran villages, the swamp, and stalactites were gone, incinerated by the unleashed energies. And the Toa Nuva had, at last, achieved their destiny — after a thousand years of slumber, the Great Spirit had awakened.

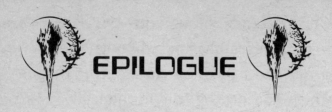

EPILOGUE

Tahu Nuva stood in the center of the great Coliseum of Metru Nui, listening to the cheers of over a thousand Matoran, among them Tanma and the Matoran of Light. Beside him stood his teammates, and nearby were Takanuva and the surviving members of the Toa Mahri. All of them could not help feeling a surge of pride in this moment — even Kopaka was smiling.

After so much struggle, so many battles won and lost, at last the quest was over. It had been dangerously close, but they had been successful. The Great Spirit was awake, the core of the universe had been cleansed of the Makuta, and balance had been restored to the universe. While none of them had seen the Mask of Life since their escape, they felt sure its countdown to destruction had stopped.

"Now this is what I'm speak-talking about," said Lewa. "This is being a Toa-hero!"

"I'm just glad we all survived," said Gali, glancing over at the Mahri. Somehow, their team seemed so incomplete without the presence of Toa Matoro, who had given his life to save the universe.

"I never doubted it," said Lewa, smiling. "As soon as we got there and saw those dark-bat losers, I knew it would be as easy as taming a Gukko bird."

"Oh, really?" said Kopaka. "Funny, you didn't seem that confident when you were trying to figure out how to steer the Axalara."

"Yeah, how many stalactites did you crash into? Three? Four?" laughed Pohatu.

"Quiet," said Gali. "Turaga Dume is about to speak."

The wise Turaga stood in his box high above and looked out over the assembled crowd of Toa and Matoran. For a moment, he was overcome with emotion and could not speak. Then, at last, he found his voice.

"My friends, we are gathered here today for a great celebration," he began. "But we must do more than honor the heroes who stand before us. We must use this time to remember all who have given their lives to bring us to this point.

"Toa Matoro, Toa Lhikan, and hundreds of other Toa whose names we may never know fought and died to keep the Brotherhood of Makuta from victory. Without their efforts, none of us would be standing here today. Without their light, shadow would rule the land."

There was a long moment of silence, then Dume spoke again. "Over one thousand years ago, the Makuta struck at the Great Spirit, casting him into a deep slumber and robbing us of his protection and guidance. For this crime, they have paid the ultimate penalty. Now, at last, we are free of them, forever."

The cheers began again then, rocking the very structure of the Coliseum. Dume made no effort to quiet the crowd. He knew this was an outpouring of happiness that was long overdue.

The Final Battle

When the noise had finally subsided, he raised his staff of office and gestured toward the Toa Nuva. "We have emerged from the darkness and into the light. And we have the six heroes who stand before us to thank on this great day —"

His words were cut off by a fleeting shadow that passed over the twin moons and an ice-cold breeze that cut through the Coliseum. Tahu glanced at Gali, confused and troubled. They had all felt something like this before, but never expected to feel it again.

"Look!" said Kopaka, pointing up to the sky. "The stars! Look what's happening to the stars!"

High above, the stars of Metru Nui were darting across the sky, spinning wildly. It looked as if the universe itself was being undone and remade at the same time. Slowly, the stars began to realign, coming to rest in a pattern both bizarre and horribly familiar. From random stars in the skies, they had arranged themselves into a shape — and it was the shape of the Mask of Shadows.

"This is impossible," said Tahu. "Why would the stars shift to look like Makuta's mask? Unless . . ."

"No," said Onua. "No, it couldn't be."

"What does it mean? What can it mean?" asked Gali.

"I think I can guess," Kopaka answered. "Radiak said the Makuta wanted Mata Nui to be awakened, but we could not guess why. Now Great Beings protect us if I am right about what has happened. . . ."

The reply came from everywhere at once. A dark, humorless laugh boomed from every stone, every star, from the ground, the sky, the ocean. Matoran huddled together in fear at the sound even as the Toa drew their weapons.

"Makuta!" shouted Tahu. "We thought you were destroyed, but if we were mistaken, we are ready to correct that mistake! Show yourself!"

The reply came in a rumble of thunder. "Show myself, you insignificant flea? Look around,

The Final Battle

Toa Tahu — I am everywhere. I am everything you see."

"What new crime have you dared commit?" yelled Turaga Dume.

"No crime, wise one," answered Makuta, his voice as soft as the breeze that heralds a storm. "Your heroes brought Mata Nui back from death . . . but before his spirit could return to his body, mine slipped in and took its place. And so when the Toa Nuva awakened Mata Nui, they awakened his body . . . with my mind."

"We have fought you before," said Kopaka, "and we will do so again!"

Makuta chuckled, sending a tremor through the Coliseum. "Will you fight the air you breathe, Toa? The ground you walk on? Understand — I no longer need to battle you in hopes of ruling the universe. I *am* the universe.

"Of course, you do have one hope," continued the Master of Shadows. "Mata Nui himself. Too bad for you that I have banished his spirit into the Mask of Life and now . . ."

The ground shook violently as a surge of energy flowed through all existence. "Now I have banished the mask from this universe. I hope you have enjoyed your fleeting moments of happiness, Toa . . . they are the last you will know for an eternity to come."

And somewhere in the endless void between here and there, the Mask of Life flew. Free of the bounds of the Matoran universe, it had turned from silver back to gold once more. It carried within it in the mind and spirit of Mata Nui, on a journey whose destination no one could know. But if anyone were able to hear the being within the mask, one statement would have been clear, ringing through the void like the tolling of a bell:

I will return.